PEDIE
GOES TO THE
AQUARIUM

KIMBERLY ARCHER

GSH

ISBN: 978-1-63821-013-9 (Paperback Edition)
ISBN: 978-1-63821-014-6 (Hardcover Edition)
ISBN: 978-1-63821-012-2 (E-book Edition)

Some characters and events in this book are fictitious. Any similarity to the real persons, living or dead, is coincidental and not intended by the author.

Book Ordering Information

Phone Number: 315 288-7939 ext. 1000 or 347-901-4920
Email: info@globalsummithouse.com
Global Summit House
www.globalsummithouse.com

Printed in the United State of America

DEDICATION

Kimberly Archer is the creator of the 'The adventures of Pedie' series. Pedie and the Aquarium is her 4th book.

The aquarium in this story is a composite of several aquariums the author visited. Aquariums are essential not only to entertain the public, but to provide an education about the endless life and beauty within. Oceans are vital to the health and well being of our planet, a source of wonder and inspiration to peoples around the world.

I would like to thank my friend Leslie Archer for all her invaluable assistance. I would also like to thank my friends Victoria Clark and Jeff Graham with whom I have visited aquariums in our travels.

Today is an exciting day at the Aquarium! It's Pirate's Day! On Pirate's day everyone gets to dress up like a pirate and is given a map to find the hidden treasure.

Pedie thinks he would be good at this, as he is a hound dog. Hound dogs have a strong sense of smell and are good at finding things.

This aquarium is located by the ocean as well as a wooded area that includes ponds and streams. There are several trails where people are allowed to walk their dogs. On Pirate's day dogs are allowed in the aquarium. Pedie is very excited to be a part of this fun day!

At the entrance to Pirate's cove everyone is given a treasure map with clues to solve to find the hidden treasure. It really looks like an old treasure map! There are 5 clues to solve. Pedie wonders what the treasure is. Everyone gathers in groups to begin the treasure hunt. It is a nice day but a little windy as it gets by the ocean.

When Pedie sets the map down to sniff at the paper the wind picks up and whisks the map away! Startled, Pedie quickly runs after the wind blown map. Luckily it lands in a small pond not too far from the edge of the water.

Pedie likes ponds, he has one at home. Pedie feels confident that he could swim out and retrieve the map but this is not an ordinary pond. As Pedie begins swimming several large colorful fish start to follow him. This is a Koi pond! Koi fish are ornamental fish with bright spots and flowing fins. Some of them are quite large, bigger than ordinary goldfish.

When Pedie sees them he feels a little scared, but the giant koi fish are only curious about Pedie. He is able to retrieve the treasure map and swim to shore. The koi fish follow him, as they think he has a treat for them. Pedie doesn't have a treat, but he thanks them for their help in retrieving the map and trots back to the treasure hunt.

This time when Pedie sets the map down to look at the clues he is careful to step on it to hold it in place. The first clue shows a picture of a school. Pedie wonders what that means.

clue # 1

Then he remembers that fish swim in schools. So he begins to look around for a large 'school' of fish. Inside the aquarium he finds a huge tank with lots of silver colored fish. There are hundreds of them all swimming together. When they turn they look like shimmering coins. Pedie wonders if these fish are part of the treasure. Pedie has solved the first clue. This is a school of silver dollar fish!

The second clue is a little harder to solve. It's a picture of a star! A star, as in the night sky? Star light, star bright, star fish! That's it!

clue #2

Pedie goes to look for a star fish in a tidal pool. Tidal pools are very interesting. When it is high tide the pools are covered with sea water. When the tide goes out sea creatures are trapped in the pools of water in the rocks. There are star fish and sea urchins, crabs and small fish. Sometimes there is even an octopus! You have to look hard to see them as they camouflage themselves.

Pedie does not see an octopus but he does find several orange and purple starfish in the tidal pool exhibit. Their colors are very vibrant! They look just like stars! Pedie is very excited to have solved the second clue!

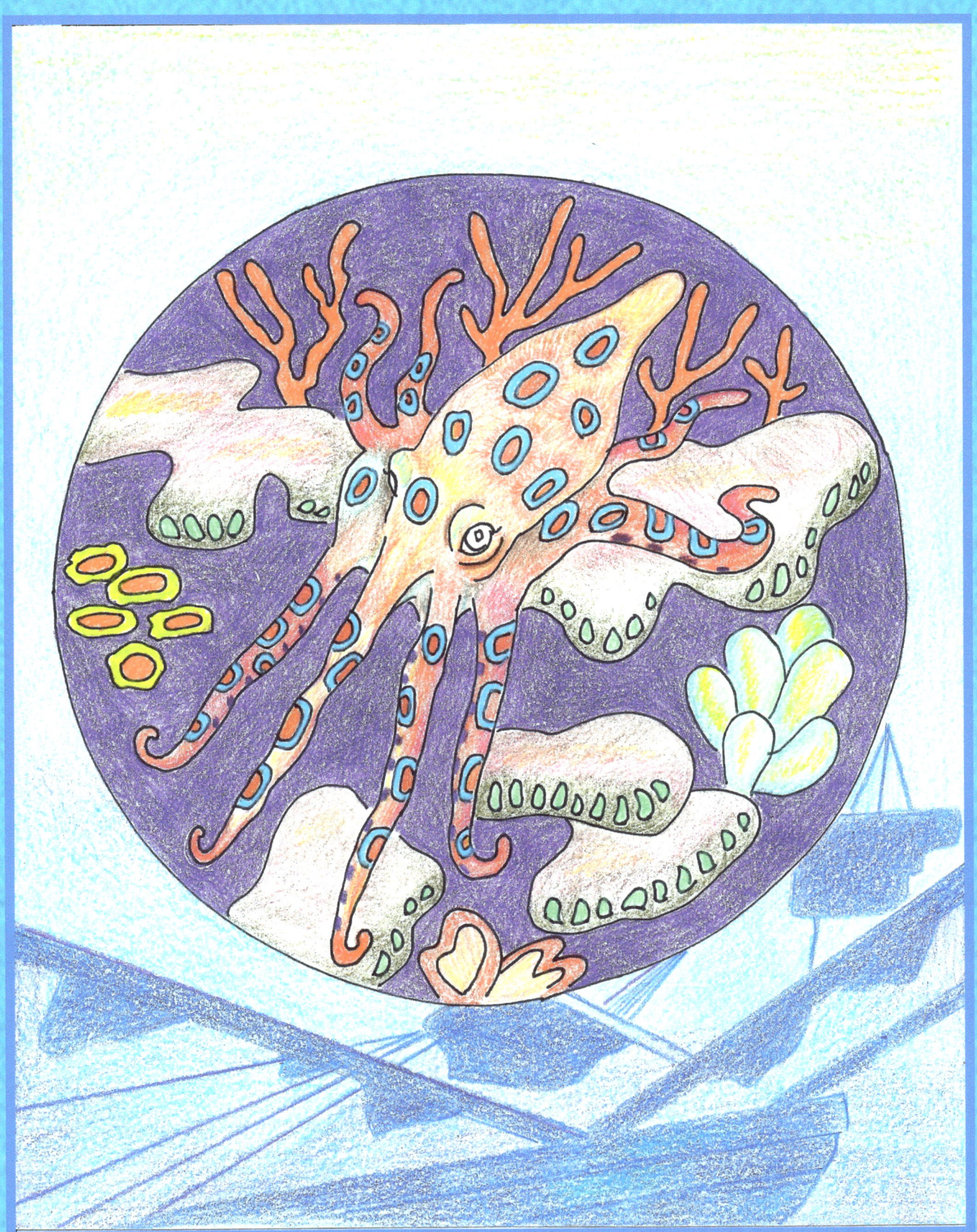

Pedie looks at the map to see the next clue. It shows a picture of a clown. A clown at the aquarium? Pedie really needs to think about this one.

He decides to walk back to the big tank, that's where the crowds are going. He thinks, if a school of fish can be called silver dollar fish, and the tidal pool creatures can be called star fish, maybe there is clown fish. He is right! There they are in a smaller tank with brightly colored sea anemones. Sea anemones are poisonous but clown fish are not affected by the poisons bards and can swim freely in the waving arms. Together they form a symbiotic relationship where they help each other with food and protection. Pedie likes their black, orange and white color.

21

Having solved the 3rd clue and enjoyed the brightly colored clown fish, Pedie looks at the map to find the next clue. It is a picture of a sandwich with a jar of peanut butter. It looks like this;

peanut butter and ? sandwich

Pedie's favorite snack is a peanut butter and jelly sandwich! Does that mean a jelly fish? Pedie wonders what they look like. He wanders through the aquarium until he comes to a tall cylinder tank where he sees unusual upside down dome shaped bubbles floating with long tentacles. They are quite beautiful and not like any fish Pedie has ever seen before. They float on the surface and move with the water. Pedie imagines they might be gooey like jam if taken out of the water. He wonders if that is how they got their name.

What he doesn't know is that jelly fish can sting with their tentacles. This is how they catch their prey, just floating in the water and stinging whatever fish swim through. They can still sting on the beach if they wash up on shore. Pedie has solved the 4th clue! Thinking about peanut butter and jelly makes Pedie feel hungry. He goes to look for a snack.

At the Pirate cove the staff is serving up walk the plank burgers and cut throat french fries. Pedie likes the fries but when he sets the map down to eat them a seagull flies by and grabs the map thinking it is a french fry. Oh no, here we go again! Pedie chases the bird until it drops the map in a different part of the aquarium. The map lands next to a large pool with a big fish swimming in it. The big fish jumps up out of the water onto a dock. When he slides toward Pedie, it looks like he is smiling! It is the friendliest fish Pedie has ever seen. It makes Pedie want to go swimming with him. Pedie thinks he could even ride on the big fish's back, but then he decides it's best not to, he needs to find the treasure!

This big fish is not a fish at all but a warm blooded mammal called a dolphin. Dolphins have to come up for air, they cannot breathe under water like cold blooded fish. Dolphins are very social and intelligent and can be trained to do tricks. A little known secret is that they also like to play keep away with seaweed in the wild!

Pedie waves good-bye to the smiling dolphin and looks around to see where he is. He is careful to hold onto the map. He still feels hungry but has forgotten about the cut throat french fries in the excitement of meeting the dolphin. Now he thinks he'd better figure out the next clue, as it is getting late.

The next clue is a picture of a horse with a saddle. Is there a sea horse? Is it big like the land animal? Pedie cannot imagine what it would look like. Maybe it lives near the clown fish and jelly fish. Pedie trots back to that part of the aquarium.

clue #5

As he looks into the different tanks of fish he sees sea turtles, manta rays, and lots of brightly colored fish in beautiful gardens. At least they look like underwater gardens. They are called coral reefs. Coral reefs are very important to the ocean and the health of the planet. Coral reefs support lots of different types of life from sea cucumbers to moray eels.

There in a separate tank are lots of freely flowing grasses. As Pedie looks into the grasses he sees little creatures with heads like a horse and bodies like a question mark. They are holding onto the grasses with their tails! They are the same color as the grasses and blend right in. One kind even looks like a dragon with sea weed growing on him. They are fascinating! The other amazing fact about sea horses is that the male sea horses care for their young babies in a pouch on their belly. Pedie is amazed at the diversity of life in the ocean.

Pedie has solved all five
clues on his map.

As Pedie makes his way back to Pirates cove he comes across a disturbing display. It is a wading pool filled with oddly shaped plastic trash floating in the water. The trash is all shapes and colors, some dirty and some barely used. Pedie wonders at the significance of this exhibit. It doesn't look like any of the other sea creatures he has seen, nothing is alive. In fact instead of a sense of wonder he feels sad and uneasy. He does not think this is a good thing.

Pedie turns his thoughts to all the different sea creatures he saw today as he walks back to Pirates cove. He thinks about the funny names some of the fish have. There were the koi fish in the fresh water pond, the silver dollar fish swimming in a school. Next there were the star fish in a tidal pool, then the clown fish and jelly fish. Why were they all called fish when they did not all look like a fish? Then he met the smiling dolphin who was a mammal. Finally there were the sea horses. They really did look like tiny horses. Pedie marvels at the wonder of it all.

Pedie realizes the treasure he was searching for is the ocean itself and all the diverse and wonderful life that lives in it.

Pedie has solved this last and most important clue.

Pedie arrives back at Pirate's cove where he and all the other pirates are rewarded with a treat of pearl drop ice cream! Pedie is happy to finally get a snack, and to have had such a fascinating and exciting day at the Aquarium!

A COLORING SHEET FOR YOU